To EAMONN —

WITH LOVE

Jim Scott

YOU ARE WHO YOU ARE, AND
THAT MAKES YOU JUST RIGHT.

Knight-time for
Brigitte

For Truman and P. Tunisia

Created, written and illustrated by Jim George.
Calligraphy by Bob Seeley.
Research and story development by Peggy George.
Edited by Lynne Piade.
Pre-Press Production by Romney Lange.

Enchanté Publishing
120 Hawthorne
Palo Alto, CA 94301

For information about Enchanté,
please call toll-free 1 (800) 473-2363.

ISBN 1-56844-040-5

10 9 8 7 6 5 4 3 2 1
First Edition

Printed in Singapore

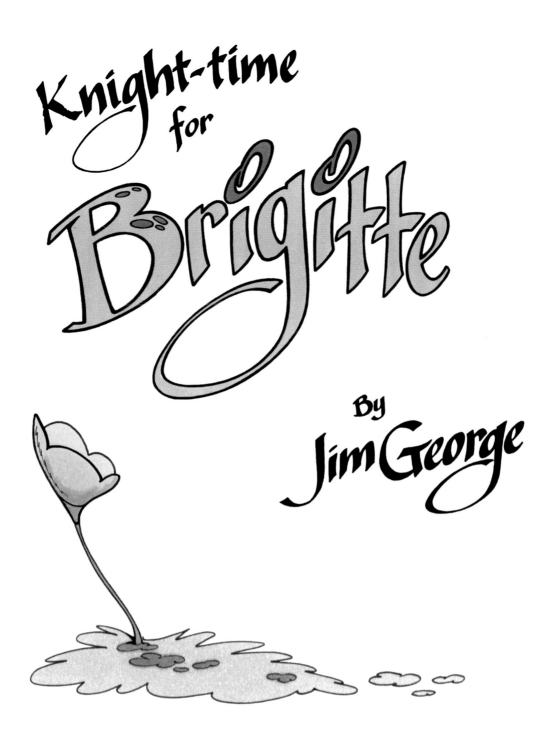

Knight-time for Brigitte

By Jim George

Enchanté

Enchanté Publishing   Palo Alto, California

In the middle of Maidenhead Meadow one night,
   when the moon was half-full and the light was just right,
Brigitte the dragon sat still for an hour
   and there, she just stared at her favorite flower.

Still as a stone she got down on her knees,
   peeked past the petals and tried not to sneeze.
She thought up a thing in the moonlight that night,
   "It is what it is, and that makes it just right!"

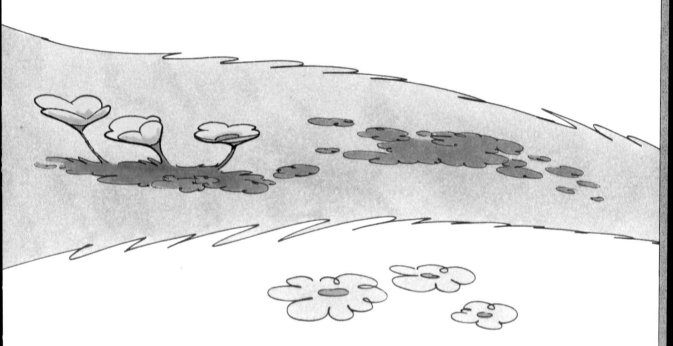

Then all of a sudden a clattering clank,
like buckets of bolts being tossed in a tank
in the bushes behind her was what Brigitte heard.
And she heard it a lot and she thought, "Oh my word!"

Out of the brush in a rush and a flurry,
came some kind of six-legged thing in a hurry.
Raving and waving all over the place,
then it slipped and it tripped and fell flat on its face.

It whumped and it thumped. It bumped into a stump.
It crumpled and slumped in a lump on its rump.

It laid there. It stayed there. It stayed very quiet.
Brigitte crept over and stood there right by it.

This was no six-legged monster at all.
It was only a two-legged man who was small.
And his poor little four-legged horse who looked hurt,
slumping there next to the stump in the dirt.

She noticed the outfit the little man wore.
This was a **knight!** She had seen one before.
He appeared toward the rear of her favorite story
of young Dragonella and dragon prince Rory.

To her, Dragonella and Rory, (her sweetheart),
flying away to the sky was the neat part.
She wasn't quite sure, "Did the knight-guy *fight*, mostly?"
She wished she had listened a little more closely.

The little guy opened his little knight-eye.
　　　Brigitte bent down to the ground and said, "Hi!"
　　As a polite dragon does, when she spoke,
　　　she puffed out a heart-shaped *"hello"* there in smoke.

"My name is Brigitte!" she said very proudly.
　　　"**And** I can **spell** it!" and she did so, quite loudly.
　　"I'm Sir Bernardo from the Castle of Ner-nee...
　　　it's too hard to spell. You can just call me Bernie."

"Oh dear," whispered Brigitte, "Oh you poor little man!
　　　You went and you bent and you dented your can.
　　And how is your horsey? The one with the chair.
　　　I know this sounds silly, but you gave me a scare!"

"I'll have you know, this is armor for battle!
　　　And that's not a chair. That's a custom-made saddle!
　　The seat comes complete with a red coffee-cup,
　　　'case a knight or his steed need a quick pick-me-up."

"And this is my knight-light to night-fight a dragon.
　　　I made it myself, I must say without braggin'.
　　And how 'bout my sword, here? I think it's quite knightly."
　　　Brigitte nodded her head then she spoke up, politely:

"**U**h...

...fighting *dragons*?" she asked as she pulled at her ear.
"Ah! Thanks for reminding me. That's why I'm here.
See, hero-type knights take a hero-type journey.
And slaying the dragon's the hard part," said Bernie.

"**I**t's right in this rule-book of knightly behavior.
Just sit yourself down, here, and do me a favor.
Open it up to page eight-seventeen,
paragraph D. There, y'see what I mean?"

Brigitte could see that ol' Bernie was right.
The dragon was slain there in plain black and white.
"But why would you do that?" she asked him quite rightly.
"How could a dead dragon make you more knightly?"

Bernie looked up. Then he looked far away.
He seemed to be sad as he started to say,
"Dragon-wise, dear, I'm afraid that success is
the only way princes can get their princesses."

"Back to the facts! Don't distract me again!
A dragon's a dragon and men must be men!
So turn right around, now, and watch what you're sayin'.
I'm a knight! You're a dragon! It's time we got slayin'!"

They started to walk. Then ol' Bern' flipped his lid.
"You call those things wings? Why you're only a **kid**!"
She held up two fingers and said, "I'm **this** many!"
(Which was only two hundred, and that's hardly any.)

Bernie was raving, "My journey's a **dud**!
Back there at the castle, kid, my name is **mud**.
Open the book to page four fifty-three
under 'Baggin' the Dragon' there, what do you see?"

"A dragon's no dragon without certain things:
ya gotta breathe fire; ya gotta have wings.
Now maybe you **can** blow a flame through your gizzard,
but **I** can't go back with a fire-breathing lizard!"

Said Brigitte, "I *do* not like feeling so small.
   I do not think that I like you at all.
And maybe my wings aren't enough for a knight,
   but they are what they are and that makes them just right!"

She said what she said there, and then just in case,
   she huffed a big puff of blue smoke in his face!

Bernie said, "Brigitte, I'm sorry! You're right!
I've been a frightfully impolite knight.
Please stick around. If I sound like a snob,
it's just that I'm not very good at my job.
I like you a lot. I did **not** mean to miff you."
"Well," Brigitte said, "then I guess I forgive you."

Bernie stood up and he shook Brigitte's hand.
Then something fell, but before it could land...

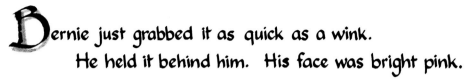

Bernie just grabbed it as quick as a wink.
He held it behind him. His face was bright pink.

He looked all around him and whistled a song.
He acted as though he had done something wrong.
"It's nothing," said Bernie, his face turning red.
(He was **trying** to sound like he meant what he said.)

Asked Brigitte, "What **is** it?" That made him cower.
He mumbled and held out... a crumpled-up...

...flower.

Go ahead. **Laugh** at me! See if **I** care,"
Bernie was waving his hands in the air.
"A knight who likes flowers! What a **dumb** thing to do!"
Brigitte said, "No, Bernie...

...I like them too."

You **do**???" Bernie asked as he stared up at Brigitte.
He couldn't believe it. He started to fidget.
"You mean you don't think I'm a rinky-dink knight?
Slightly off-white? Not quite alright?"

People in castles (at least back in ours)
don't think it's right for a knight to like flowers."

Brigitte sat down and she gave it some thought.
"Maybe it's not in that book that you brought,

but...

If **I** were a knight (and thank goodness I'm not!)
I'd be a knight who liked flowers a lot!"

Bernie just stood there. His tongue was all tied.
He'd never felt quite so delighted inside.

When all of a sudden from out of the sky,
a big ball of bright yellow fire flew by!
It showered the flowers that Brigitte loved most
with badly-aimed flames and it turned them to toast.

Bernie hopped backward and fell on his seat.
What could drop glops of such hopping-hot heat?
Brigitte was standing there shaking her head.
"I think it's my big brother Bartlett," she said.

"Get away from my sister, you knobby-kneed geek!"
Bernie just shivered there, too weak to speak,
'cause big-brother Bartlett made Brigitte look small.
Bernie fell over curled up in a ball.

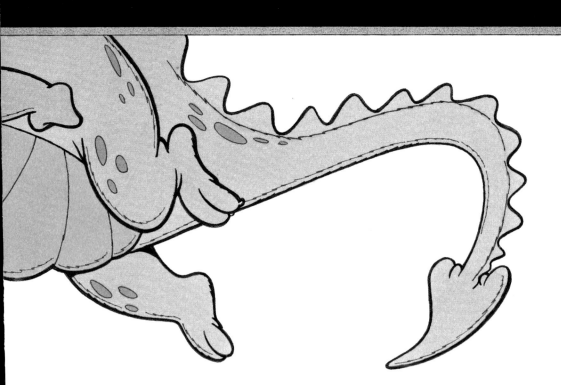

Bartlett let fly with a new spew of fire.
  Brigitte ducked down as the flame shot right by her.
It barely missed burning poor Bernie real bad
  and fried some more flowers. Now **Brigitte** was mad.

"Quit it, you twit!" Brigitte spit in a snit.
  "I do not need all this **nonsense** one bit!"
But Bartlett was too busy saving his sis'
  to stop whopping Bernie and listen to this.

So Brigitte did something she knew wouldn't fail
  to get his attention:

She torched his *tail!*

"*Ow!*" shouted Bartlett. He stopped right away.

"If you don't **mind**, I have something to say.
He is what he is. He's a very nice knight.
If I need to be saved, I will **ask** you, alright?"

She puffed out two smoky-blue hearts up above them.
   (That's how dragon sisters tell brothers they love them.)

Bartlett just stood there all puffy and pale.
   His sister had blistered the tip of his tail.
"**Humph!**" he harumphed as he wandered away.
   She was right and he knew it. What else could he say?

Then Brigitte asked Bernie if he was alright.
  "I'm afraid I'm all **wrong**," Bernie said, "for a knight."
He sat very sadly, his chin on his hand.
  "It seems that you still do not quite understand.
I have this problem. I hate to keep naggin',
  but **I** am supposed to be slaying a dragon!"

"Of course, **you** won't do 'cause I **like** you too much.
  I **can't** slay a friend who likes flowers and such.
Bartlett's too big ... and besides, he's your brother.
  And frankly, off-hand, I can't think of another."

"A hero-type knight would have done it by now,
  dragged back a dragon. (Heaven knows **how!**)
The King and the Queen and the Princess would cheer:
  'Hooray for our hero-type knight, here! Hear! Hear!'"

"Well, I have no dragon; not even a half.
  And when I get back to the castle, they'll laugh.
The King and the Queen and the Princess will smirk:
  'Away with this **zero**-type knight! What a **jerk!**'"

"How sad," Brigitte said, as she sat on the ground.
Both of them sat there just looking around.
They sat and they sat and they sat there some more.
They sat there so long that their bottoms got sore.

And after what seemed like at least half an hour,
Bernie got up and gave Brigitte his flower.
"This is for you. I won't need it again.
You are what you are, and you're lucky, my friend."

"I'd better get back. They'll be waiting for me...
...or waiting for someone that I *ought* to be."

Brigitte looked down at the flower and sighed.
    She felt like a part of her died there inside.
She couldn't let Bernie just ride off like that;
    back to his castle and then get laughed at.

She wanted to help him. But what could she do?

    Then...

...she got an idea. Brigitte said, "I'll go **too**!
I've got a plan, Bernie. Don't give up yet!
I can stay still as a stone, don't forget."

"We'll fool all your friends and pretend that you **slayed** me.
It'll be **fun**! You could **drag** me there, maybe!
I'll act like you whacked me one...here, on the head.
Then back at the castle they'll think that I'm dead!"

Bernie was breathless. He hopped off his horse.
He ran up to Brigitte and shouted, "Of **course**!!
And through all the hero-type yakkity-yak;
no one will notice you slip out the back!"

Brigitte kept thinking of every detail.
Their time was at hand and the plan mustn't fail.
"I'll lay on my back so they won't see my wings.
(I know. It's just one of those silly **knight** things!)"

They took two big sticks and made sort of a slider,
longer than Brigitte and just a bit wider.
A custom-ized, Brigitte-sized, flat-bedded sled,
for a dragon to drag on and not hurt her head.

Then off they all hauled toward the Castle of Ner-nee,
on a path that would make a fake hero of Bernie.
They moved through the moonlight and made up a song,
and sang it ten times as they toodled along.

They came to a castle carved right out of rocks,
　　　held up by trees that were growing in blocks
　of chalky bedrock in a lake with a dock.

Brigitte asked Bernie if this was the place.
　　　Bernie said, " no ," . . . and he picked up the pace.

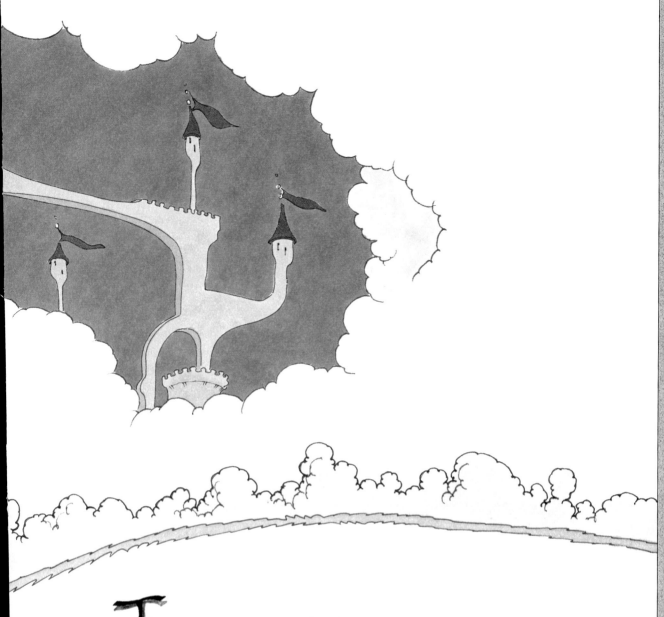

They came to a castle clear up in a cloud.
Brigitte said, "**Wow!**" and she shouted out loud:
"Is **that** where you live? Way up there in that tower?"
Said Bernie, "No. Ner-nee's another half-hour."

They walked till they spotted a sign that read: "**Ner-nee.**"
"We're nearly here. In that clearing," said Bernie.
Brigitte could tell at a glance he felt small,
'cause the castle just didn't look fancy at all.

The walls were all leaning. They all leaned a **lot.**
"It must have been lovely at one time," she thought.

How sad. Now it seems like it's starting to rot.
Except for that flower on top in the pot."

"Oh…I put that there," Bernie said with a sigh.
"No one would know if I put it up high.
I almost got caught by the King and Queen's daughter
one time when I climbed up to give it some water."

"The place needs a face-lift, alright. That's a fact.
The draw-bridge won't work and the tower is cracked."
But Brigitte looked past all the cracks in the tower.
All she could see was the beautiful flower.

NER-NEE

Then came a call from the King's Commandant:
   "Who the heck goes there and whadda-ya-want?"

"I'm Sir Bernardo. I'm here with a dragon.
   Go tell the King. Then please bring me a wagon."

Brigitte was glad to get off of the sled.
   "Get ready to start playin' dead," Bernie said.
"Still as a stone," Brigitte whispered with pride.
   She closed both her eyes and looked just like she died.

From out of the gate came a great crowd of shouters,
      shouting quite loudly and then shouting louder:
"**Bernie's a hero!** Just look at that wagon!
      He went out and bush-whacked and brought back a dragon!
He'll marry the Princess now, that's what I think!"
      Brigitte gave Bernie a quick little wink.

Into the castle they carted their treasure,
      with everyone cheering, "Hear! Hear!" with great pleasure.
Thumping on thumpers and clanging a bell;
      and the King and the Queen and the Princess said...

" ...well... "

"The hair could be pinker, I think," said the Queen.
"It's not very big... for a dragon, I mean."

All of the cheering "Hear! Hear!" got real quiet.
The Princess walked over and stood there, right by it.
"The tail is a tad bit too wide. And besides...
I'm *not* sure the spots are the same on both sides."

The King mumbled something that nobody heard,
more of a burp or a slurp than a word.
He might have been clever, he might have been kind,
but the King just had too many things on his mind.

"And that **green**!!" said the Queen. "Well, that green is too **green**!
Why, that green is the *ugliest* green I have seen."
The Princess was pouting. The King turned away.
"Some **Knight**!" said the Queen. "Have you **nothing** to say?"

THINGS
TO DO:

Bernie looked up and surveyed the scene.
　　He looked at the Princess, the King and the Queen.
"You are what you are; and I guess that's alright,
　　but...
　　　　I am what **I** am. What I'm **not** is a **Knight**."

"Brigitte, we're leaving!" Then everyone froze.
　　'Cause a puff of blue smoke had just huffed out her nose.

NER-NEE

Brigitte just smiled and she opened her eyes,
and then she stood up to her full dragon size.
She folded her arms and she looked down at Bernie.

Then...
...they proudly walked out of the Castle of Ner-nee.

The three of them —Yup! Bernie's horse was there too—
held their heads high. They knew **just** what to do.
They toodled right back and they toodled back proud,
singing their toodling song way too loud.

When they got back to the meadow that night,
  and Brigitte went left and Bernie went right,
neither one wanted the journey to end.
  "What will you do?" Brigitte asked her new friend.

"I know who I am . . . way down here in my heart.
  It may not be much, but . . .
                    that's a pretty good start."

"We'll meet in the meadow again some sweet night,
    when the moon is half-full, like it was here, tonight."
They waved their good-byes till they walked out of sight.

They were who they were. And that made them...

...just right.